The BAd BUNNiEs' MAGIC SHOW

MINI GREY

To HILARY DELAMERE and Agents of Magic everywhere

TONIGHT THE GREAT ~~CANCELLED~~ HYPNO

FEATURING SUCH TRIUMPHS OF PRESTIDIGITATION AS: THE TIGER TRANSFORMATION. THE RAPID KNIFE DISPLAY. THE VANISHING LADY. AND THE APPEARING CEPHALOPOD.

SIMON & SCHUSTER
First published in Great Britain in 2017 by Simon and Schuster UK Ltd · 1st Floor, 222 Gray's Inn Road, London, WC1X 8HB · A CBS Company · Text and illustrations copyright 2017 Mini Grey · Moral rights asserted All rights reserved · HB 978-1-4711-5759-2 PB 978-1-4711-5760-8 · Printed in China 10 9 8 7 6 5 4 3 2

Ladies
and gentlemen,
we have to announce

A SLIGHT CHANGE OF PLAN.

Due to circumstances
beyond his control,
the *Great Hypno*
has been detained,
and instead we present

a SURPRISE NEW ACT...

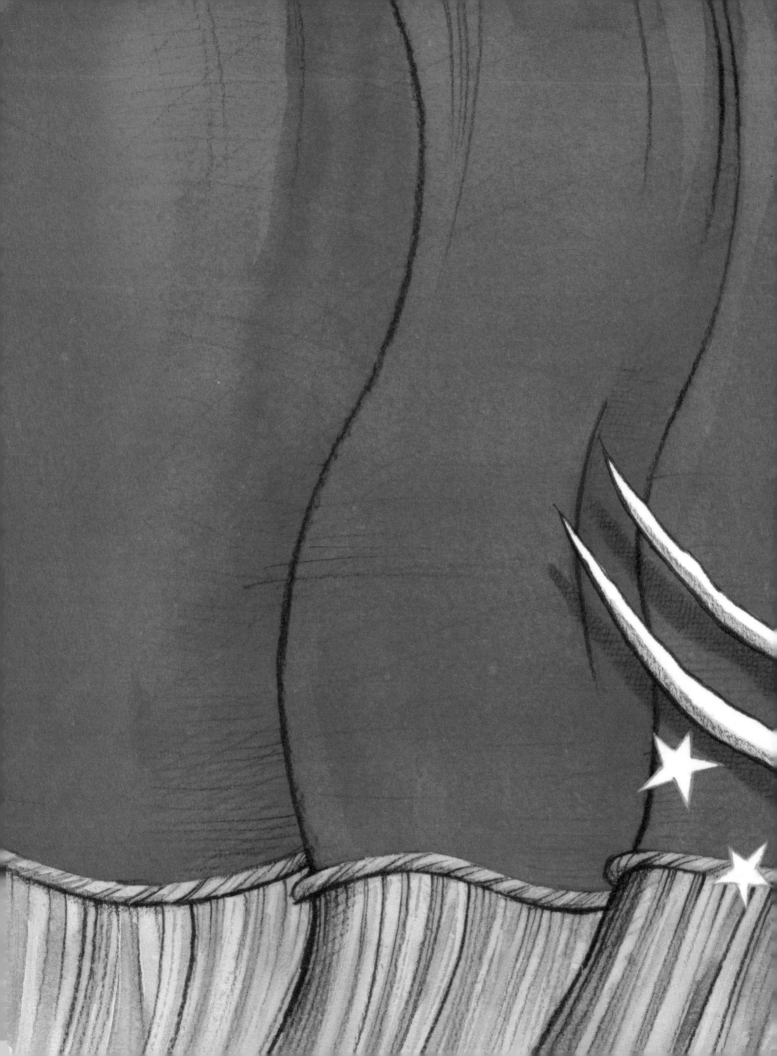

Ladies and Gentlemen,
it is our pleasure
to introduce. . . .

Tonight's show
will be **fast**
and **dangerous**
and not for the
faint-hearted.

And now . . .

LET THE
SHOW
BEGIN!

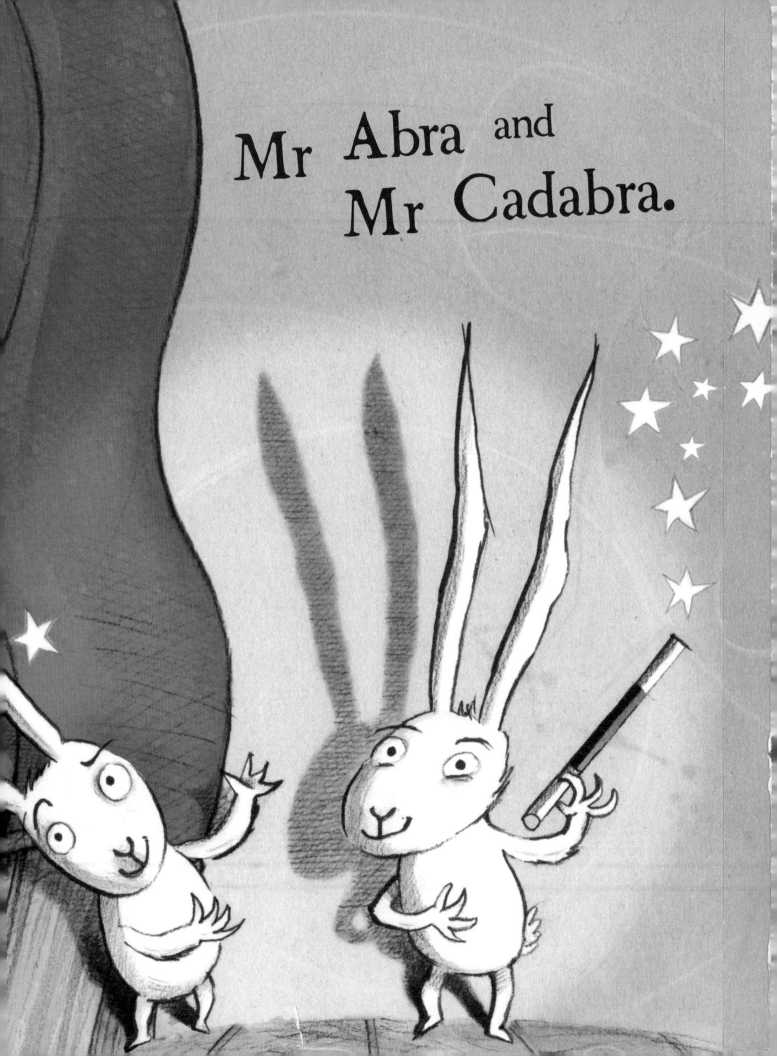

Mr Abra and Mr Cadabra.

For their first trick
Abra and Cadabra
will have some fun

with

this small goldfish.

HEY PRESTO!

ABRA and CADABRA
will demonstrate
SLEIGHT OF PAW
and
NERVES OF STEEL
with a display of
RAPID
KNIFE-THROWING.

AND
NOW

Abra
and
Cadabra

present

THE
BIRDCAGE
TRANSFORMATION.

Hold onto your seats while **Abra** and **Cadabra** saw the lovely Brenda

in half.

HEY PRENDA

And now, sshhhh,
a bit of *Escapology*
and don't make a sound
as I,
the lovely
Brenda,
pick my way
through these chains
and padlocks.

And now, Ladies and Gentlemen, for their GRAND FINALE, as they count down from TEN, Abra and Cadabra would like you to put any WATCHES, PEARLS or

GOLD JEWELLERY you are wearing
into this sack for their final
DISAPPEARING ACT!

10 ...

9 ...

8 ...

Ladies and Gentlemen,
allow me to finish this 'show'
by blasting these (ahem)
BRAVE BUNNIES
into
KINGDOM
COME

from the

CANNON of DOOM

5...4...3...2...1...

It's time for a feast at the old Carrot and Canary . . .

I think I may have
a plan . . .